MIGHTY MIKE

SAVES A School Bus

By Kelly Lynch   Illustrated by Casey Lynch

magic wagon

visit us at www.abdopublishing.com

For Rocky, who can fix almost anything. –KL
For Nate –CL

Printed in the United States of America, North Mankato, Minnesota.
092010
012011
♻ This book contains at least 10% recycled materials.

Written by Kelly Lynch
Illustrations by Casey Lynch
Edited by Stephanie Hedlund and Rochelle Baltzer
Cover and interior layout and design by Abbey Fitzgerald

Library of Congress Cataloging-in-Publication Data

Lynch, Kelly, 1976-
   Mighty Mike saves a school bus / by Kelly Lynch ; illustrated by Casey
Lynch.
        p. cm. -- (Mighty Mike)
   ISBN 978-1-61641-133-6
 [1. Repairing--Fiction. 2. Helpfulness--Fiction. 3. Community life--Fiction.] I.
Lynch, Casey, ill. II. Title.
   PZ7.L9848Ms 2011
   [E]--dc22
                                                        2010016266

The rain was coming down in big, wet drops. It turned the dirt into mud and the mud into gooey muck. Mighty Mike was working on this gooey, mucky day and he was covered in mud. As you can imagine, Mighty Mike was feeling mighty low.

Mighty Mike plopped down in the mud and gave a big sigh. Then, he decided to do something he hadn't done in a long time. He decided to go home early.

Mighty Mike had just gotten home. He was looking forward to dry clothes and a warm bowl of soup when the phone rang.

"Mike!" cracked a concerned voice. "This is Principal Fullerton. The school bus broke down and we need your help! It's full of kids and they need to be at the spelling bee in two hours!"

Oh bother, Mike thought. *Whenever someone needs help, they call me! Why me? Especially on such a rainy day!*

Mighty Mike was about to tell Principal Fullerton he couldn't help, but he started thinking. *People call me when they need help,* Mike thought. *And I think I know why. It's because I'm reliable. People know they can count on me!*

"I'll be there as soon as I can!" Mighty Mike shouted into the receiver.
When Mighty Mike arrived at the broken-down bus, everyone was happy to see him, especially the bus driver, Rocky.

"We don't have much time to get to the spelling bee," Rocky told Mike. "I've tried everything, but the bus just won't go."

Mighty Mike grabbed his tools and pulled on his rain jacket. He opened the hood of the bus and started wiggling wires as the rain poured down.

"Everything looks okay, Rocky," Mike said as he peeked around the hood of the bus. "Try starting it."

Rocky turned the key and the bus growled and grunted but wouldn't start.

"Hmmm," said Mighty Mike. "I don't see anything wrong. Are you sure it's not out of gas?"

"I'm sure," answered Rocky. "I fill the bus every morning before my route."

Mighty Mike poked his head back under the hood as the rain plopped down. He checked the fan belt, the fuel filter, and the fuel pump.

"I still don't see anything wrong," Mike said to Rocky. "You're positive it's not out of gas?"

"I'm sure, I'm sure," repeated Rocky. "Like I said, I fill the bus every morning. Keep looking."

Mighty Mike checked the alternator, the distributor, and the radiator.

"Rocky," Mike hollered from under the bus, "there is nothing wrong with this bus! It must be out of gas!"

"No, no, no!" roared Rocky. "I'm sure it's not out of gas." The rain was really coming down.

Mighty Mike checked the water pump, the oil pump, and the power steering pump. But, he still could find nothing wrong with the bus.

"Rocky," Mike said, "are you *sure* you put gas in the bus this morning?"

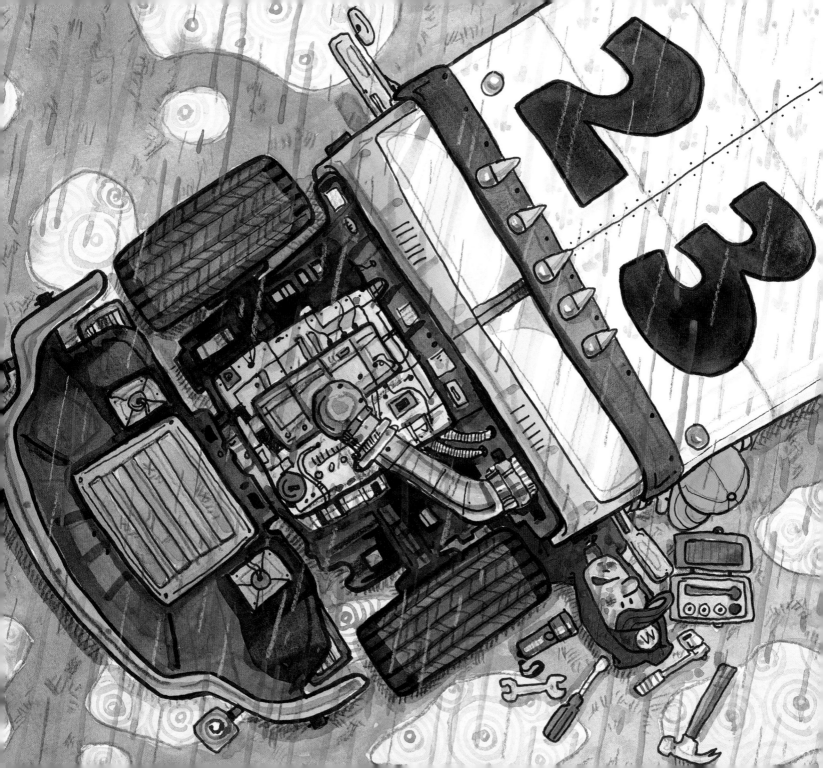

"I'm positive!" Rocky replied. Then he thought for a moment. "Well, I think I did," he said with just a hint of doubt. "If I didn't, I meant to. I mean, I don't think I forgot."

"Rocky," said Mike sticking his greasy, oily, sopping wet face around the corner of the bus, "what does the gas gauge say?"

Rocky glanced at the gas gauge and his face turned bright red. "Well, uh," he stammered. "It's a little below the E."

After putting some gas in the bus, it started right up. Rocky and the kids roared off to the spelling bee. A greasy, dirty, soaking wet Mighty Mike leaned against his truck and looked up at the thick, gray sky.

Just then the rain stopped, the clouds opened and the sun broke through. Mike smiled. Sure, he could have been snoozing in his favorite chair. And yes, he was greasy, oily, and wet. But Mighty Mike didn't mind being greasy, oily, and soaking wet if it meant he was reliable!

Glossary

alternator - an electric generator that produces a current to run a vehicle.

distributor - a device in a vehicle that directs a current from the induction coil to the various spark plugs of an engine in their proper firing order.

fan belt - a belt that drives a cooling fan together with a dynamo or alternator in a car engine.

fuel filter - a filter in a vehicle's fuel line that screens out dirt and rust particles from the fuel.

gauge - a measuring device.

power steering - a steering system in a vehicle with engine power that helps apply more turning power to the steering wheel by the driver.

radiator - a device in a vehicle that moves heat from the engine to keep it cool.

reliable - trustworthy or dependable; people can count on you.

What Would Mighty Mike Do?

• Why is Mighty Mike upset at first about the school calling him?

• Why does Mighty Mike decide to fix the school bus?

• How does Mighty Mike feel when the school bus is fixed?